Mary's Pets

Clive Scruton

Lothrop, Lee & Shepard Books • New York

One bright, sunny day
Mary was in the yard
looking for her pets.
Where had they all gone?

Mary whistled, and
guess who came running,
with a waggy tail
and a silly grin?

Sam, the dog.

Who suddenly pounced from the tree, with a saucy, bouncy purr?

Who came creeping along, ever so slowly, his small head peeping from his house on his back?

Who hippety hopped and twitched her ears as she popped up from behind the old rambling rose?

And who called out,
"Maaa...ry, Maaa...ry!
Well, of course it was...

Who played with Mary that sunny day? Sam, Flip Flop, Fluffy, Henry, Topsy, and, of course, Mary's little lamb!